SAVE THE
PLANET!

Sometimes his
BRIGHT IDEAS end
in DISASTER, but he
always learns from his
mistakes.

What can YOU
do to help stop
climate change?
LOTS!

Read this book for some
BRILLIANT PLANET
SAVING IDEAS.

Meet the
Characters

← Me, Max

Nish →

← Tessa

Lily →

To BB, with many thanks for many things — TA

OXFORD
UNIVERSITY PRESS

Great Clarendon Street, Oxford OX2 6DP
Oxford University Press is a department of the University of Oxford.
It furthers the University's objective of excellence in research, scholarship,
and education by publishing worldwide. Oxford is a registered trade mark
of Oxford University Press in the UK and in certain other countries

First published 2020

British Library Cataloguing in Publication Data

Data available

ISBN: 978-0-19-277513-9

1 3 5 7 9 10 8 6 4 2

Printed in India

Paper used in the production of this book is a natural,
recyclable product made from wood grown in sustainable forests.
The manufacturing process conforms to the environmental
regulations of the country of origin.

Graph paper: Alfonso de Tomas/Shutterstock.com

Friday was the day I realized the world was

going to end. I was in the playground at

lunchtime, talking with Nish and Tessa about

the **BIG** climate change protest we'd seen

on TV the night before.

'Did you see those people dressed up as

polar bears?' asked Tessa. 'They must have been uncomfortable in those costumes.'

'Yes, un<u>BEAR</u>able!' laughed Nish. 'One bear bumped into a policeman, and they both fell over. You don't see that on the nature documentaries!'

I couldn't help smiling, but the protest had <u>rattled</u> me. I couldn't forget the huge banner they'd carried, saying:

TEN YEARS TO STOP CLIMATE CHAOS

We'd all heard about climate change before, but it seemed to be getting more urgent, and the more I heard, the worse it sounded. Nish wasn't helping.

In 10 years people will all have to walk on stilts because there will be floods everywhere and the wildlife will suffocate because all the cows' farts will be trapped in the atmosphere.

'Maybe I should start stashing honey under my bed now—if all the bees die, what will I put on my toast?' said Tessa.

'Someone will think of something!' replied Nish. 'They're working out how to grow our food in test-tubes. Anyway, 10 years is ages away.' The bell rang for the end of breaktime. Time's up . . .

All afternoon it was **really** difficult to concentrate in lessons. Was 10 years

4

really ages away? I wasn't great at maths, but didn't think it added up to a long and happy life for us. My parents say I worry too much, but shouldn't EVERYONE worry about this?

Future Max 2030

Dry bread, no honey

Worn-out umbrella

New t-shirt with rising oceans

Face mask to block cow farts

With beard

Super unfashionable wellies

At the end of lessons, I went straight

home. I wanted a chat, but Dad was busy

looking after my little sister Lily, and it was

one of the evenings when Mum's out at work.

After tea, I went up to my room. The thing is,

the longer you fret about something without

talking about it, the worse it can feel. I tried

to take my mind off things

by playing Gerbil Hero! on

the computer, picking my nose,

and practising my duck faces in the

mirror, until Dad told me it was time

for bed—and by then I was too tired for

a <u>big talk.</u>

I fell asleep fairly quickly, but worries

started to bounce round my head like a

demented frog in a bucket, and I had

a full-on nightmare.

I woke, heart hammering, covered in sweat, breathing hard, feeling hot and cold at the same time. My hands were clutching my duvet as tightly as if I was hanging on to the edge of a cliff. I slowly loosened my grip, and stared hard at the ceiling, which was real and solid.

AHH!

Dad opened my door, wearing his dressing

gown. 'What's going on? You were shouting

. . . are you alright?' He said this in the hissy

voice people use when they get

up in the middle of the night,

like a cross between a yell

and a whisper. I told him

about my climate

change nightmare.

It had started weird rather

than bad, with me trying to

hoover the house with a lawnmower, and

the carpet turning into fake plastic grass—but

then it had become TERRIFYING.

Skeletons wrapped in cling film chased me,

and I fell through tree-rooty things into

a fire, but in the fire I was drowning, not

burning. I was shouting for my life, and that's

what Dad must have heard.

He got me a glass of water with a slice

of lemon in it, because it helps chill

me out; he calls it 'Lemon-Aid',

which isn't as funny as he thinks

it is. We talked a bit until I felt calm

again, and I reckoned I'd be able to go back

to sleep. Dad promised we'd have a **proper**

chat in the morning.

z z Z Z Z

He's good at calming me down from bad dreams.

A few years ago, I had them a lot. They weren't about **climate change** back then, but were always **strange** and scary. I'd been getting "worried that there might be something wrong with my brain, but Dad had told me it was because of my **strong imagination**, which is actually a great thing to have. He'd said if I tried to worry less and use my imagination for good

things, then the nightmares would stop. He'd

been right—until now.

    I got up later than usual the next day.

In the kitchen, Mum and Dad had finished

their breakfast, and Lily had almost finished

throwing hers about.

Morning, love!

said Mum, picking a piece of

jammy bread out of her hair.

'Sorry you had a rough night. Ready

for some breakfast?'

'I'm not hungry,' I replied. I took a deep

breath, and told Mum everything.

So, in 10 years, cows' farts will kill us all!

'We don't have much time left when you think about it. You're already quite OLD but I have LOADS more life to live!'

Mum was looking at me seriously, but kindly. 'Oh, Max. There's lots to think about for sure, but let's not panic. We can spend some time learning more about this stuff together, and see if there's anything you can do to make a difference.'

'I'm just a kid, trying to mind my own business!

What difference am I going to make?' I retorted.

Across the table, Dad looked up from

his laptop, raising his eyebrows.

Boring money stuff

Mega volume hair serum for men

Dad's dream car

'You don't <u>ALWAYS</u> mind your own

business, Max—we haven't forgotten about the

16

time you posted a photo of your headteacher on

the internet, asking if any other school wanted to

give him a job. I bet he hasn't forgotten, either!'

'I was only trying to help his career!' I

protested.

'Hmmm. Never mind that. Anyway ... come

and look at this.' He turned the laptop

so we could all watch. He'd found

a video of a speech by a Swedish

girl called Greta, who didn't look

that much older than me.

At the end, Dad closed the laptop, and I sat

back, thoughtfully.

She'd said a lot of pretty intense stuff,

but it made sense. She'd said that hope came

when people started to **take action**,

and that really stuck in my mind. I needed

some hope right now!

'Thanks Dad, that was super-

interesting,' I said, reaching for the

cereal with a little smile. I was thinking more

about what I'd seen on the video. Kids across

the world were scared like me, but were

trying to change things by plotting, planning,

and kicking up a fuss. I reckon I could be

pretty good at that...

It was time to MAKE A PLAN.

A Plan for the Planet!

I needed to get clued up, so decided to do

some online research. I found images of forests

cut down, oceans full of plastic, and shrinking

glaciers, which all made me really anxious again.

I couldn't think straight. Also, I found that

doing research makes me really hungry. Who

knew?!

I decided to take a biscuit break.

Besides, it was time for

which is one of my favourite TV

programmes—I try to watch it every

weekend. It was the usual hilarious mix

of games, music and cartoons . . . but this

time there was something else too.

Wilf was launching a new competition,

an environmental project for schools

called Wilf's Wonderful World Award.

Interesting! I turned the volume up . . .

'Hey, hey, hey! We want to find the

keenest, greenest school in the country!'

Wilf was saying. 'Could it be yours? We want

you to make eco-improvements at your

school, keep a record of what you achieve,

and tell us about it! It's easy to enter . . . just

download an entry form from our

website and get busy! There's

a fantabulous prize for the winner, of

course—a special trophy for you to keep,

and an amazing surprise reward for everyone

in the school! And guess what . . . we'll film

a special edition of the show at the wacky

winning school!'

This was it! Nobody could change the

whole world at once, but making things

happen at school would be a great start.

I was going to enter this competition. Ideas

started to flood my mind. Imagine if we won!

My school on TV . . . and I'd get to meet Wilf!

I sat back and pictured myself accepting

the award.

Practice makes perfect, so I went into the

bathroom and stood in front of the mirror.

I emptied the toothbrushes from the mug on

the washbasin, and

held it up proudly,

like a trophy.

In the other hand, I gripped a shampoo bottle like a microphone. I started to speak to my reflection, but it didn't come easily. Finding inspiring words was HARD, especially when I realized I was holding the bottle upside down and the lid wasn't on properly.

I was wiping strawberry shampoo off my T-shirt when Mum knocked on the door.

KNOCK

KNOCK

Are you OK, love? What are you doing? Are you on the phone? I sighed, and unlocked the door.

'No. I'm just thinking about my **Plan for the Planet.** I'm going to start changing things on Monday. Wait and see!'

Mum turned her head and looked sideways at me.

Er... OK. Just don't get into trouble.

27

'Remember just the other week when you changed the school assembly music, and got a detention for it? I don't want you getting another one!'

'I was just trying to cheer everyone up. My tunes were so much better—everyone thought so!' I explained.

'Well, the headteacher certainly didn't. Anyway, try to behave! You can start by picking up those toothbrushes.

And why does everything smell of

strawberries?'

On Monday, I was up early for breakfast, ready to put Phase One of the **Plan for the Planet** into effect. I was going to tackle car *pollution* and Mum and Dad were about to get involved—although they didn't know that yet!

'Have you got the car keys? They aren't here!' said Mum, looking underneath magazines and papers near the hook where the keys usually hang.

'I haven't had them!' Dad shouted down the stairs.

They didn't ask me, which was lucky, as it meant I didn't have to lie. I knew where they were, but wasn't telling . . .

'If you can't find the keys, maybe you should walk, or get the bus?' I suggested helpfully. 'It's <u>much</u> better for the environment

not to drive. We all need to do our bit.'

Mum gave me a look. 'Not now, Max! If

you want to help, start looking for the keys!'

Dad came into the kitchen. 'Where have they

got to? We're going to be late!' he exclaimed.

'I definitely left them on the hook!' shot back

Mum, running her hands through her hair.

It was time to come clean. 'Er ... I *might*

have seen them,' I said. 'I think maybe they

were in Lily's toy box, *perhaps.*'

'What? Why didn't you say? How did they

end up there?' demanded Dad, making a

beeline for the box in the corridor. I followed

him, and helped turn out all Lily's toys in search

of the keys. When we'd emptied the box with no

success, I was super worried.

No keys

No keys

NO keys

NO KEYS!!!

'What the hell are you playing at?' Dad

shouted, kneeling amongst a pile of scattered toys.

I took a deep breath. 'I don't know where they are . . . but I *did* put them in there,' I confessed, looking at the floor. 'I thought maybe if you couldn't drive you might see that walking or getting the bus is fun, you know?'

'Honestly, Max! How could you be so stupid? Where have they gone?' yelled Mum.

This really wasn't going well. 'I'm sorry!' I

muttered. 'They WERE in the box. Lily must

have put them somewhere!'

Mum and Dad started searching furiously

again. I tried to help, but didn't know where

to start. I tried to imagine myself in my sister's

head. If I were a loopy toddler and found

some shiny keys, where would I put them?

They weren't in any of the places I imagined,

which shows I don't have a toddler's brain, I

guess. (That's probably a good thing.)

I needed a quiet think,

so I went to the toilet.

I lifted the seat, and there

were the keys! I felt a huge

flush of relief, even though I hadn't yet

relieved myself, or flushed. **I found**
them! Lily dropped them
in the bog! I shouted, and gritted

my teeth, because I knew

what I had to do next.

I rolled up my sleeve,

GRRRRRRR.

knelt down, and scooped the keys out of the bowl, which was thankfully clean.

Mum and Dad rushed in. 'At last!' cried Mum triumphantly, snatching the dripping keys from my hand, and rinsing them under the tap.

'We're off. You can be sure we'll have a lot more to say about this tonight, Max,' added Dad ominously. 'And wash your hands, now!'

'Erm . . . hang on, can I have a lift? I'll be late for school!' I said, sheepishly.

Mum whirled round. 'You've got a

nerve!' she exclaimed. 'NO, you cannot—

get walking!' And with that, they bundled

Lily out of the house and slammed the door

behind them.

After all that, I was <u>seriously late</u> for

school and was sent to see the headteacher,

Mr Costive. As soon as he saw me, he looked

up at the ceiling, scratched the scraggly

tufts of hair above his ears with a sigh, then

frowned at me. I started to explain about

my **Plan for the Planet** and the

competition I was going to enter on behalf of

the school, but he cut me off.

'I don't care how you get here,

or how **environmentally**

unfriendly it is, just don't be late

again. It is **unacceptable!**

Now, get to your lesson.' He gestured at

the door with a lanky arm.

What a rubbish morning—having a row

with my parents and being called to the

head's office was not the start I'd wanted.

I moaned about it to Nish and Tessa at

breaktime.

Nish responded with his impression

of Mr Costive. He stuffed his mouth with

sweets and waved his arms about, muttering

'Unacceptable! Unacceptable!'

I smiled. 'Well, he certainly didn't want

to know about my **Plan for the**

Planet, and nor did Mum and Dad. They

just don't get it—but we're going to show them

that we can make a change!'

'Hang on . . . *we?*' said Nish. 'What are you

going to get us into this time, Max?'

'We're going to enter Wilf's Wonderful

World Award!' I announced, dramatically.

'Didn't you watch it at the weekend? We can make the school really green, and we could be winners!'

They were excited to hear about the competition, but Tessa had doubts. 'I'd love us to win, but do you really think you can persuade people here to get involved?'

I'm going to try, Tess! I declared, firmly.

We are going to try.

I didn't dare say any more about my Plan

for the Planet to Mum and Dad

after that. I was on total best behaviour at

home, as there was a school trip coming up,

and I was worried they wouldn't let me

join in. I was super relieved when they said

I could go, because I really <u>LOVE</u> trips.

They're like the best bits of school—hanging

out with friends and finding out interesting

stuff—but without all the boring school bits.

z^z^z

This one was to the museum, and I was <u>really</u>

looking forward to it, because they have

DINOSAURS!

The day of the trip,

I was woken up by the

sound of rain hosing

onto my window . . . and

 was shocked when I saw the time.

My alarm hadn't gone off, and I'd overslept.

Panicking, I raced into the kitchen, where Mum was washing up. 'There you are. Didn't you hear me call you? You need to hurry up if you're not going to miss the school trip!' I looked out of the window; the rain was so heavy it seemed to make the house rattle. I looked at Mum pleadingly.

'Come on—I'd better take you. Don't you

dare touch the car keys, though!' she said,

with a wink.

As we arrived at school my friends were

already there, waiting for the coach to the

museum. 'Hi Max—nice comfy car journey?'

grinned Tessa. 'Yes, what happened

to all the eco-talk?' added

Nish.

I couldn't help feeling a

bit guilty. 'Er, it was raining

loads, and I was late, and my

mum was driving anyway . . .' I mumbled.

'Ha! You've been banging on about

climate change all week, and as soon as the

climate ACTUALLY changes, you

jump in a car!' he crowed.

'That's not what climate change means,

whiffhead!' I protested, but he

carried on chuckling as we boarded the bus,

and set off.

smug

stuck in the middle

Thankfully, Nish had stopped going on

about it by the time we got to the museum.

There was so much to see, but everyone's

favourite was the dinosaurs. However many

pictures you see, standing next to actual

fossil skeletons lets you imagine how big and

awesome they really were. It was

mind-blowing

to learn that birds were closely related to

dinosaurs—I'd have to tell Dad that if he

took me birdwatching again!

49

I was also really interested in a display

talking about how the dinosaurs died out,

which reminded me of all the stuff I'd heard

about animals and plants going extinct

nowadays. I wondered what amazing species

might be for the chop if things didn't change,

and it made me even more determined to

make sure things <u>DID</u> change.

On the coach ride back to school, I was

telling everyone about the competition. 'So,

we could all be on TV!' I explained. There

were squeals of excitement. 'Oooh, we'll

see Wilf in real life!' someone shouted. The

back row of the coach started singing the

Wilf's Wacky Weekend Wig-out

theme tune and everyone joined in, until the

teachers called for order.

'Hey, everyone's really into the competition!' said Nish. 'You might actually be onto something here for a change, Max!'

'So, what do we do first?' Tessa asked.

'I'll think about it, Tess. Watch this space!' I replied, tapping my head, which was starting to fill up with ideas.

By the time I got home after the trip, I had

a strategy for making the school greener and

impressing Wilf.

I spent the evening making a leaflet on

Dad's computer, and printed off loads of

copies on his printer. They looked great!

JOIN THE CAR-FREE CAMPAIGN

Come to school by bike, bus or walk instead.

Less pollution!

 It's fun!

We could win Wilf's Wonderful World Award AND GET ON TV!

HELP THE CLIMATE

SAVE OUR FUTURE

54

I took them into school the next day and showed my friends. 'I want to start a **Car- Free Campaign!**' I said. 'We can give these out at home time, and try and get kids to walk or cycle.'

'What if it's raining?' grinned Nish cheekily.

'I'll get an umbrella. Simple!' I retorted.

'Giving out leaflets sounds boring,' complained Tessa. 'Will anyone take any notice?'

'We've got to try!' I said. 'Nothing's going to happen unless we get together and take action. Come on, what could go wrong?'

They reluctantly agreed to give it a go. So, after school we stood at the gates, and gave leaflets out to kids and their parents as they left. It was fun—Nish and Tessa admitted they'd quite enjoyed it.

Most kids took leaflets, although Matt McDonald and his stupid mates screwed them up and threw them back at me,

or made paper planes out

of them. I got angry at that,

but Tessa persuaded me to ignore them

and concentrate on handing leaflets to the

less annoying kids (and, anyway, I managed

to rescue most of the crumpled ones).

We leafleted again the next day,

and the next.

Tessa even made

a little banner to hang

on the school gate.

Mr Costive made us take it down, but we put it back up again when he wasn't looking.

We started to see more kids walking, cycling, or scootering to school. A few moaned at me that it was my fault their parents made them walk to school. 'Remember the competition!' I said. 'If everyone walks, everyone wins!'

I knew we were getting somewhere when even Danny Belter said he supported the campaign. Danny is the grumpiest lad in the whole school, but he was glad we'd given

him an excuse to walk to school. 'Anything's

better than listening to my dad's terrible

music in the car every day,' he told me,

and almost smiled!

6

I'd stuck a **Car-Free Campaign** leaflet on the fridge door at home, cunningly recycling a bit of stray jam from Lily's high chair to act as glue. Mum and Dad weren't pleased about the jam, but they read the leaflet anyway.

my leaflet

'Now we know

why there's no ink in

my printer!' Dad declared,

waggling the leaflet at me.

I braced myself for a telling-off, but he said,

'So, you've started a campaign. Well done—

I hear there are fewer cars outside the school

gates these days. Other parents are talking

about it too.'

'Yes. Better than hiding busy people's car

keys,' added Mum, giving me a look.

'Anyway, we've decided to join the campaign and start cycling to work!' he smiled. 'We were wanting to keep fit anyway, and cycling is good exercise. Also, we'll save money on petrol.'

'Amazing! I'm really glad you're going to join in!' I said, buzzing that my parents had actually been inspired by me and my friends. Kids were really changing things!

Dad spent the next few days looking at cycling websites. He called it 'research', but it seemed to me he was mostly watching videos

of bike races, and looking at pictures of

super expensive racing bikes.

Dad subscribed to 'Pedaller's

Weekly', which is a nerdy cycling magazine.

I flicked through a copy he'd left lying about.

Most of it was pretty boring, with pictures of

mudguards and brake levers or whatever, but

there were two whole pages on

'How To Choose The Best

Skintight Shorts'—I hoped Dad

wouldn't read that one. Even worse was an

article called 'Bare Biking—Cycling

Naked and Free!' which I *really* hoped

he wouldn't read. I hid the magazine under a

pile of newspapers, just in case.

It wasn't too long before Dad came home with a bike. It was bright yellow, with two seats. 'Er . . . What's this? Are you both going on the same bike?' I asked. 'It's a tandem, Max,' beamed Dad. 'And yes, we are. Two for the price of one!'

I hadn't expected this. 'Who's going to sit at the front and steer?' I asked.

'**I am!**' said Mum and Dad at exactly the same time, then looked at each other, laughing. 'We'll see tomorrow, when we do our first bike trip!' continued Mum.

I was eating breakfast the next morning when they both came into the kitchen, and the sight made me choke on my Corny Snowflakes. They were wearing identical outfits, and it was clear that Dad *had* read the article about skintight shorts.

'You look like you're wearing bin bags.

Really *small*, tight bin bags,' I spluttered,

aghast.

'Don't be rude. These are aerodynamic

suits and the very best cycling

attire,' said Dad proudly.

Now come on, time to go!

As we left the house,

they put on cycle helmets,

and I saw to my **horror**

that each had a sticker on

the side which said 'HIS' and 'HERS'.

'So we don't get them

mixed up,' explained Dad,

noticing my mortified expression.

'We'll ride with you to school,' said

Mum. 'It's on the way to Lily's nursery

anyway.' I scurried ahead as quickly as

I could, but they mounted the tandem,

squeezing Lily into a little seat on the back,

and wobbled after me.

Nish was waiting for me on the corner,

and his eyeballs nearly popped out of his head

when he saw the tandem. 'Er ... Max ... is

that normal? And what are they wearing?'

he asked, waving nervously at my parents.

'Don't encourage them!' I hissed,

grabbing his arm and pulling him

onwards. We walked

off quickly together, the

tandem not far behind.

My parents were clearly

enjoying the ride—Dad in particular was

having a great time, sitting at the back

waving his arms about and yelling, 'Look,

no hands!' at passing pedestrians. It was so

embarrassing! Still, it could have been worse

I suppose—they could have read the article

about naked cycling . . .

Mum and Dad finally weaved off

towards Lily's nursery, and we continued to

school. I sighed with relief. 'Don't worry,

they're not going to follow us every day!'

I reassured Nish.

'Good job!' he replied. 'I couldn't handle

that every morning. Why do parents have

to be so embarrassing? Even so, it's really

cool that they're so into cycling. You've

made a change, Max!'

He was right; despite the embarrassment,

I felt a flush of pride. More importantly, Mum

and Dad weren't the only ones; lots of kids

were walking or cycling to school (though

in normal clothes!) and the route to school

was already nicer to walk, with fewer cars.

Kids in my class were talking more about the

environment too, and were excited about the competition.

My friends and I needed to work out what to do next, so we held a strategy meeting at breaktime. We sat on a bench sharing a maxi-pack of crisps, and trying to come up with ideas.

'You keep saying the planet needs more trees, Max,' said Tessa, thoughtfully

(and crispily). 'Well, there's loads of space on the edge of the playing field. We could ask if we could plant some trees there.'

'Genius, Tessa!' She'd got my <u>strong</u> <u>imagination</u> working now. I jumped up, scattering a few stray crisps in the process. 'We can tie labels to the trees to write worries about the environment on . . . and write what we're going to do about the problems. It will be INSPIRING—a Forest of Hope!'

'It sounds like hard work to me!' said

Nish, grabbing the crisp packet. 'Anyway, the

teachers might not allow it.'

'Why don't you take it right to the top

and get Mr Costive to agree? Then the other

teachers will have to help,' Tessa suggested.

So I spent lunchtime trying to track down

Mr Costive, which wasn't easy. I saw him go

into an empty classroom, but

when I followed him in, he

wasn't there—it was as if

he'd vanished into thin air! Later, he was in the

dinner hall, so I ran over.

'No running in the hall!

Unacceptable!' he scolded. 'Don't bother

me now, Max. I'm going into the kitchen to ...

er ... check they've got enough spoons.'

I waited outside the kitchen door

till the end of lunchtime, but

he didn't reappear. If I didn't

know better I'd have thought

he was avoiding me.

I told Nish and Tessa about my failure to

find him.

'I wouldn't be surprised if he **is** avoiding

you,' said Nish. 'I don't think he's

forgiven you for the time you

went to talk to him about your

plan to redecorate the classrooms and left

painty handprints all over his door.'

 'But this is important!' I

retorted. 'And if he won't approve

our plan, we're just going to have to

sort it out ourselves. Let's just give *ourselves* permission! We could hold a tree-planting ceremony tomorrow lunchtime. We'll invite our whole class and make it happen.'

Tessa stopped me. 'Hang on! Before you go round inviting everyone, you need some actual trees! Where are you going to find those?'

I had to admit she had a point.

A Forest of Hope

without any trees would be **pretty**

hopeless. Maybe Mr Costive could help

after all—he could get the trees, and I would

sort out the advertising.

I wrote a note to Mr Costive inviting

him to the ceremony, and asking him to

buy some trees (I thought fifteen

would do). I popped the note under his

office door, and then got busy telling my

classmates.

Enthusiasm was lower than I'd hoped.

Kids loved the idea of winning

the competition, but weren't

so keen on going outside in the

cold to dig holes.

I was worried that the ceremony

would be a flop, so asked my friends to

help spread the word. Nish came up with a

suggestion. 'Why not get the local newspaper

to take photos? Then everyone will want

to be there to get their funny faces in the

paper!'

I thought that was an unusually good

idea from Nish—if we got in the paper, the

campaign would get a real boost. As it was

impossible to get hold of Mr Costive, I'd

have to phone the newspaper myself. How

hard could it be? 'You two tell everyone

the newspaper's coming, and I'll handle the

phone call!' I said, and ran off to find a quiet

corner to make the call.

I knew they wouldn't take a call from a

kid seriously, so I decided that the obvious

thing to do was to **impersonate**

Mr Costive. First of all, I needed to

try to sound like him. He talks a bit like he's

got something in his mouth all the time, so

I tried speaking while holding a piece of

chewing gum in one of my cheeks. His voice

is deeper than mine, so I had to drop my

tone. I practised by talking at the wall, until I

thought I was getting close.

Finally, I put some toilet paper over my phone to disguise my voice even more, and dialled the number.

'Hello, I'm the headteacher at Jedley School. We're having a special tree-planting ceremony tomorrow. Do you want to come?' I mumbled.

'Er . . . good afternoon,' responded the reporter. 'Sounds interesting . . . what are you planning?'

'We're making a Forest of Hope.

All the nice children will be there. Well

behaved. 12 o'clock on the school field.

You could get some great photos.'

'Well, it is the sort of thing we cover,

and it's a quiet news week, so . . .'

'Don't worry, we won't be noisy,'

I assured him.

He laughed. 'Great! We'll send a

photographer at 12. And your name is . . .?'

I almost said 'Max', but remembered

at the last minute, so actually said

'Maa . . . sssster Costive.'

'OK, see you tomorrow, Master

Costive!' said the reporter, and hung up.

Phew! I'd done it—result!

The next day, I was in lessons, pretending to listen to Ms Perkins, but actually thinking about the tree-planting plan. (To get away with this, I sat near the back, with a SERIOUS face on.) Would the ceremony go well? Would the photographer turn up? I was wondering whether Mr Costive

had done his bit and bought the trees, when

there was a sharp rap on the door and Mr

Costive himself burst in. At once, everyone

sat up straight. I was probably about to find

out . . .

Max Twyford! A word, right now!

he bellowed, pointing a

bony finger at me like a

gun. It's bad news when

teachers use your full name, especially when they want 'a word'. I followed him to his office, where he closed the door behind us ominously.

As I expected, he had more than just 'a word' to say. 'What on earth do you think you're doing, inviting the local paper here TODAY to watch me plant trees that we don't have—unacceptable!' he ranted. 'You can't dream up crazy ideas and just expect them to happen here!'

88

'Why not? I tried millions of times to come and talk to you about this, Sir,' I protested. 'It's not my fault I could never find you! I left you a note so you'd know we needed your help. Anyway, it's <u>NOT</u> crazy, it's a great idea.'

'I can't believe your cheek! There are proper procedures, you know. A reporter and photographer are coming <u>this afternoon</u>, thanks to your meddling!' He paused, shaking his head angrily, and stared at me in silence for quite a while. I couldn't actually

remember seeing him this angry before (and

I'd seen him get angry a lot). I needed to say

the right thing to calm him down, and was

trying to think quickly . . .

But before I could say anything,

he sighed through clenched teeth, and

continued. 'Unfortunately it would look bad

 for the school to cancel now,

so I'm going to have to

permit this hare-brained

scheme. Your class can come and do this silly

ceremony for the cameras. Anyway, I need to

find a spade and buy some trees—goodness

knows where from.'

Despite Mr Costive roasting me, I was

trying hard not to smile. The school was

going to get the Forest of Hope

after all! 'Try Big Blossoms Garden Centres,

sir,' I suggested helpfully. 'They have

branches everywhere.'

'Don't try to be funny, Max—you're still in

my bad books, and you **won't** be coming to

the ceremony, by the way. Detention for

you! Now, get out . . . I've got trees to find.'

So, when all the rest of my class filed out

excitedly later that day to help plant the

trees, I was kept behind. Mr Costive made me

pick up litter in the playground, which

he called 'a good job

for an environmentalist'.

As I trudged around picking up sweet wrappers with cold fingers, I could see the ceremony in the distance through the fence, and really wished I was there.

After school, I went straight out to look at the trees with my friends.

'We all helped plant a tree and they took loads of photos—it was great!' said Tessa. 'It really sucks that you weren't there, though,' she added quickly, seeing my disappointment. 'You made it happen, Max.'

'Mr Costive was annoying, though,' said Nish. 'He just stood there going on about it like it was his idea, while we planted the trees and made our promises. He just wants to look good in the newspaper.'

I sighed. 'You know what—it doesn't really matter. He can say what he likes, but we all know it was down to us. And, most importantly, we got our Forest of Hope! It's great that all the other kids were into it too. We're making progress!'

Nish was reading the promises my class

had written on the labels tied to the trees,

and started to snigger. 'They won't be printing

these in the paper!' he said. I went over to

look.

I promise to stop deliberately blowing off in my brother's room, to stop air pollution.

I promise to eat pizza instead of cabbage, to save the plants.

I promise not to do a wee in the sea when I'm on holiday.

Hmmm. There was still quite a lot of work to do, it seemed . . .

'So, it's looking good for the competition

then?' asked Tessa as we walked home from

the school field.

'We've got the **Car-Free**

Campaign and the **Forest of**

Hope . . . but we need to do more if we

want to win,' I insisted. 'So, what next guys?

Any ideas?'

Nish spoke up. 'I'd like a **campaign**

against homework—everyone

would be into that!'

'How's that going to help **save the**

planet?' I scoffed.

'Well . . . it would save paper!

Think of all the trees that are cut down

to make our boring workbooks!'

he said, triumphantly.

5ax2b
=
BORING!

'Even better, what if we campaign for no lessons at all when it's cold like this?' suggested Tessa, pulling the hood of her coat up. 'I thought it's meant to be spring, but I'm <u>freezing</u>! Think of all the energy wasted trying to heat the classrooms. We'd be better off at home . . . or they could take us on a trip somewhere warm.'

'Come on, be realistic!' I said, as we stopped on the corner where we'd go our separate ways. They both sniggered.

'Realistic! That's good, coming from you, Max!' laughed Tessa. 'See you in the morning!'

As I walked on home, I thought about what Tessa had said. She had a point—our school **does** get really cold. It's an old building (even older than Dad!) and when it's freezing outside, it's not much better inside. The heating doesn't work well, so everyone complains, and we're sometimes allowed to wear coats indoors.

I needed to get my **strong**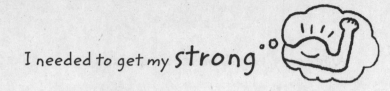

imagination working on the problem.

I remembered when Dad took me on a

special camping trip—it was one of those

summer memories that never seemed to fade.

We'd put up our tent by a lake, and watched

swifts and swallows swooping low over the

water while Dad told me the names of all

the hills on the horizon. In the morning we'd

boiled tea on our little stove and had breakfast

without getting out of our sleeping bags. I'd felt

super cosy, which gave me an idea . . .

So, the next day, I stuffed my sleeping bag

into a holdall, and took it with me to school.

I'd thought of a way I could use it to show

everyone that there were ways to be warm at

school without turning the heating up. If my

idea caught on, it would really help with the

competition entry!

After assembly, I quickly popped into the

toilets, and got into my sleeping bag. I had

to undo the bottom bit of the zip a tiny bit

and push my feet out so I could walk, and then zip up so that only my head was sticking out. I made a mistake though, by forgetting to go to the toilet first. Having a wee from inside a sleeping bag isn't easy ... I fiddled with the zip and tried various techniques, but in the end I had to take the whole thing off, do my business, and then put it all on again.

I'd need to adapt my design so I could wee easily, unless I wanted to wear a nappy underneath the bag (which I *didn't!*).

It was lesson time, so I emerged from the toilets. Movement was slow, as I could only take little shuffly steps, but already I felt warmer. Maybe a bit of that was me blushing, as kids in the corridor were laughing and pointing. 'Why are you walking around in a sleeping bag, weirdo?' one shouted.

'Er . . . you mean a <u>Totally</u> <u>Warm</u>

Nope

Insulating Tube!' I retorted. They

laughed even more, but I shuffled on.

When I came into the classroom there

was more sniggering, but I just sat in my

chair. Our teacher, Ms Perkins, gave me one

of her looks. 'Max, where have you been?

And whatever are you wearing?'

'It's a TWIT, miss!' I replied.

'It stands for Totally Warm

Insulating Tube.

It's a new idea I'm testing instead of a coat because it's so cold'.

She didn't look impressed. 'Hmmm . . . OK for now. But don't let it distract you. Everyone else—settle down, and let's make a start!'

I felt really warm all through the lesson. It was tricky to sit upright, though, as I felt like I was slipping off the chair all the time. It was also hard to write in my workbook, as I had to unzip the top of the bag as little as possible to keep the warmth in, and poke my

writing hand through the

gap.

   I was relieved when

the bell rang for breaktime. Everyone else

rushed out towards the playground. I slid off

my chair, and shuffled after them as best I

could, but I was soon left behind. One thing

I'd have to improve with the TWIT was

that it was

S L O W

to get around in. Stairs were especially

tricky—going up involved jumping a step at a

time, and going down meant bouncing on my

bum, which hurt.

When I finally got outside, there wasn't

much I could join in with. Playing football

was out of the question; Nish suggested

I could be a goalpost, but I didn't fancy

that. I left them to it, and shuffled off.

Even if I couldn't have fun myself, I was

entertaining everyone else; kids clustered

round me, giggling. **'It's Max the**

maggot!' someone shouted, and

everyone laughed even more.

'Whiffheads! You're all just

jealous because I'm toasty warm!' I replied.

'Farty warm, more like!'

yelled Matt McDonald, and I blushed again,

as in fact I *had* **guffed** in there earlier,

and had to undo the zip a bit for fresh air.

Suddenly, a few kids grabbed both ends of the

TWIT, lifting me right off the ground,

and started to swing me from side to side.

It was sort of fun at first, but soon I

started to feel sick.

'Stop or I'll

puke!' I shouted.

'Oi! Put him down!'

I heard Tessa's voice, and then Nish came to

grab me and slow down the swinging. Cackling

like idiots, the kids dumped me on the ground,

and Tessa and Nish helped me to my feet.

'Thanks guys!' I muttered. I was dizzy but

at least I wasn't going to puke.

'Hmmm. When are you going to stop being

totally embarrassing?' asked Tessa. 'We can't

bail you out all the time, you know.'

I shuffled inside to unzip in the corridor.

Maybe they had a point. Trailing the

TWIT behind me like a big popped

balloon, I went back to the classroom early,

feeling grumpy. Ms Perkins was already there,

and looked up from her desk as I came in.

'Had enough of your sleeping bag?' she

asked.

'Yes Miss. It sort of worked, but

also didn't work at all. I was

really warm, but it got in

the way of everything!

I suppose I'll go back to a boring old coat.

But—what if EVERYONE brought

in a sleeping bag tomorrow? We could zip

them all together, and it would be like a

ginormous sleeping bag keeping the whole

school warm!'

'Well, we certainly need a warmer

building . . . but I don't think sleeping bags on

the walls are the answer!' she smiled. 'Now,

lessons start in a few minutes, so put your

coat on and get ready.'

I sighed and went back to my seat. I spent the rest of the day half-listening to the teacher while trying to think up more campaign ideas. I wasn't sure what to do next, but it certainly wouldn't involve wearing a sleeping bag to school again . . .

The next day, Ms Perkins found me after

assembly. 'Your . . . er . . . TWIT yesterday

got me thinking,' she announced. 'You were

warmer when you were insulated by your

bag, because your body heat didn't escape.

This school needs something similar—a warm

layer to keep heat in, so we'll need less energy to heat the place. I did some research, and there IS some money we can apply for to insulate the building. I'll talk to Mr Costive and we'll look into it. I'll let you know how it goes!'

Now, this was promising! If we could insulate and save energy, that would be a mega boost for Wilf's Wonderful World Award.

At the end of the day Ms Perkins called

me over, smiling broadly. 'Good news. I've just

been speaking to Mr Costive . . . we've applied

for the insulation money, and it's looking

positive! I didn't think it would be that easy,

but we should be able to get the whole school

insulated. No more coats or sleeping bags

needed indoors next winter.'

FANTASTIC! This meant we'd

done enough to enter Wilf's competition! I

rushed straight home after school, wanting

to get everything out of my head and onto the entry form. I sat down and read the form. The first section was easy—'List your school's achievements here,' it said.

I started to write:

At Jedley School we have made a Plan for the Planet, with lots of brilliant strategy. We started a Car-Free Campaign, where we persuaded people to walk or bike, and now there's less traffic and pollution and everyone loves it. Next we planted a Forest of Hope, with trees for the wildlife and as a place where people can think positive future thoughts. We're also insulating the school so we will use less energy and won't need to wear stupid things to be warm.

It actually sounded quite impressive when I'd written it down—I hoped Wilf would agree!

The next section was harder. 'Why is your school special, and why do you deserve to win?' I had to think about this for AGES, and in the end I came up with this:

I don't really know if our school is special, because it's the only one I go to. But we've really done our best to change things here, and we don't want to stop! We deserve to win because we love Wilf, we care about the planet, and we would all look great on TV!

The next morning, I showed Ms Perkins my completed form, as a teacher had to sign it before I could send it off. She read it carefully, and I started to worry she'd pull out her red pen and start marking it. (I had probably made some spelling mistakes.)

'You've been busy—if only you put this much effort into your homework!' she grinned. 'Of course I'll sign it. In fact, I'd like to add a few of my own words too, and I'll even post it for you. How about that?'

I handed the form over, hoping she wouldn't lose it—once she lost the classroom keys, and Mr Osman the caretaker had to climb through a window to let us in.

Anyway, I wouldn't need to buy a stamp,

and Wilf should get the form tomorrow!

As soon as I found my friends, I couldn't

wait to tell them the big news.

'Guess what! I got Ms Perkins to sign, and

now it's done!'

Nish looked puzzled. 'What are you

on about? Are you collecting teachers'

autographs now?'

'No! You're missing the point again! The

COMPETITION!' I explained. 'I

finished the entry form, and she signed it, and

sent it off! *And Ms Perkins says the school*

is going to be insulated. The **Plan for**

the Planet is working!'

'Congrats, Max!' said Tessa. 'Let's hope

Wilf is impressed.'

'Look, we should celebrate!' I said. 'I

want to thank you for the help you've given

me, and for sticking by me, even when I've

been a pain. Come to mine on Saturday and

I'll cook us a feast!'

On Saturday, after watching **Wilf's**

Wacky Weekend Wig-out

as usual, it was time to start preparing my

celebration meal.

I'd hoped my parents might be able to

help me, but Mum had gone out with Lily

before I'd had a chance to ask her . . . and

Dad was no use, because he was ill in bed

upstairs. It was down to me!

I searched the kitchen for ingredients,

but there wasn't a lot to choose from. I really

wished I'd asked Mum and Dad for help, but

it was too late now . . . After raiding all the

cupboards, this is what I found:

- Two lettuces

- An onion

- A bag of frozen peas

- Four carrots

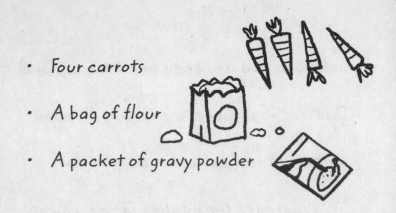

- A bag of flour

- A packet of gravy powder

There were herbs growing in a pot by

the door, which Mum and Dad like to use

sometimes (usually when they're trying to

make dinner look posher, like when their

friends come round). I picked

a big bunch to use.

I looked online for

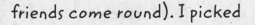

a recipe using these ingredients, but found

nothing. I settled on making a pie, which is

easy because it all just goes in one big dish.

I chopped the onions and carrots, and

put them in an oven dish with the peas. Then,

I sprinkled on gravy powder

and herbs, and poured hot

water on top, stirring it

all together. This made

a vegetable sauce, which

would be the main part of the pie.

Next, the topping. I pulled leaves off

the lettuces and spread them out so they

were floating on top of the sauce, and

then added another layer of leaves.

The packet of flour fell on the floor, but

I managed to scoop most of it up with a

dustpan and brush, so didn't waste much.

I tipped the rescued flour into a bowl, and mixed in some marge from the fridge to help stick it together (I'd seen Dad do this when making apple crumble). I spread the flour and marge mix over the top of the lettuce leaves.

All done. It didn't look much like most pies I'd seen, but there was a lot of it—we wouldn't go hungry!

All the preparation had taken longer than expected. Tessa and Nish were due to come round any minute. I put the pie in the microwave and set the table.

The doorbell rang, and there stood

my friends. 'Hey! What's for dinner? I'm

starving!' said Tessa, striding into the house.

'I haven't eaten all day to make sure I had

space!'

'Well, you're in for a treat! Welcome to Max's pop-up restaurant! Take a seat, ladies and gentlemen, and get ready for a **planet-friendly feast!**' I proclaimed.

'What are we having?' asked Tessa. 'Please say it's chicken nuggets!'

'Oh no, it's all vegetarian!' I replied, hesitantly. 'You see, eating less meat and dairy things helps fight **climate change**. It's really important, Tess.'

'This is the cows' farts thing again, right?' asked Nish. Tessa's face fell.

'What's wrong with nuggets?' she demanded. 'I don't think chickens even fart, Max.'

'It's about more than animal farts,' I explained. 'Rainforests are cut down to make land for farms, you see, and ...'

PING! The microwave interrupted. Dinner was ready! I took out my culinary creation, setting it down on the table.

'VOILÀ! Lettuce pie!'

I announced with a flourish, trying to ignore

the fact that it hadn't come out quite as

I'd hoped. The sauce was a funny colour, the

lettuce had shrunk to a stringy gloop, and the

flour had formed into a chalky white rubble.

'What's in it? It looks weird.' asked Tessa,

prodding at it sulkily with her fork.

'Umm . . . it's the taste that counts.

Try it!' I urged. They both gingerly took a

spoonful, and sat there chewing in silence.

Nish spat his mouthful out onto the plate.

'I'm sorry, Max, but this tastes like **actual**

farts. I'd rather eat my own toenails.'

'It's not that bad!' I spluttered. 'You're

just fussy, Nish'.

'Oh yes it *is*,' grimaced Tessa, spitting

out her mouthful. 'Have some yourself

and see!'

'Er ... I'm not really hungry,' I

stammered. 'I had a big lunch, you see ...'

'Come on, Max!' she scolded, passing me

a fork.

I had to try some. It was lumpy and much

too watery, except for the topping which was

lumpy and much too dry. The lettuce tasted

rubbery but also gritty, and the onions were

still raw. Sheepishly I spat my mouthful out

too, managing to miss my plate and hit the

table.

'Well, so much for your feast!' said Tessa,

glaring at me. 'I'll stick to chicken nuggets.'

I sat there, head down, deflated and hungry.

It was obvious that my celebration meal had

been a total disaster. We sat around the table

in silence, staring at the sludge on our plates.

'Well, we've got to eat something!' said

Nish, getting out his phone. 'My mum always

has loads of food in her freezer.

I'll call her and see if she has anything we can eat. Don't worry Max, it'll be vegetarian.'

Nish's mum saved the day! She only lives round the corner, and she said we could go round there to eat. Soon, we were in her kitchen, tucking into a yummy range of Indian food—spinach and chickpea curry, onion bhajis, and warm flatbreads. We ate until we could eat no more, and sat back in our chairs, sighing with satisfaction.

'That's better! I'm sorry my pie didn't work out, guys,' I said. 'And thanks, Mrs Gupta—this actually is a feast!'

'Better than eating toenails, eh?' said Nish. 'You should give Max some cooking lessons, Mum!' and we laughed.

At that, my strong imagination started to

kick in. Nish's mum is a brilliant vegetarian

cook, and loves talking about food. I had an

idea.

Onion Bhaji

Popadom

Samosa

'Hey, Mrs Gupta, how about coming into

school to show everyone how good planet-friendly food can be?' I suggested.

'I don't think that's allowed, Mum,'

muttered Nish, quickly. 'You can't just turn

up at school! Mr Costive wouldn't like it.'

Oh, never mind him!

I would love to do it!

I get on very well with

Ms Perkins. I'll ring her and

make arrangements, Max.

141

Over her shoulder Nish was shaking his head, and Tessa also looked unconvinced.

Time was moving on. 'My mum will be back by now. I'd better go,' I said. 'Thanks loads for the food, Mrs Gupta!'

As expected, Mum was in at home, but I didn't get a warm welcome. 'Where have you been? And what's been going on?' she demanded. 'Look at the state of this kitchen!'

'I had to go round Nish's, and didn't have

time to clear up after cooking.' I explained.

'Cooking?' exclaimed Mum. 'Who let you

cook? It looks like you've had a food fight!

You can start cleaning this up RIGHT

NOW!'

On Sunday morning, I was up late after a

tiring evening of kitchen cleaning. I tried to

get hold of Nish and Tessa to see how they

were, but neither replied to my messages—I

guessed they must be busy. I was wondering

what they were up to, and

I was worrying about the

competition application.

Was it any good? I didn't know. I

felt bored and flat.

'Why don't you come with me and Lily

to town, instead of moping around?' Mum

asked, ruffling my hair. 'I'm sure you've got

some pocket money to spend. Don't worry,

we'll go on the bus!' Well, I had nothing

better to do . . .

In town, Lily was pointing at everything in the shops, burbling 'Buy me! Buy!' Mum usually gives in pretty quickly and buys her a cheap toy to keep her quiet. I remembered seeing pictures of oceans polluted with plastic and thought I should get involved— it was my sister's future too, after all! 'You don't want any of this plastic junk, Lily!' I told her, as she sailed past the shelves in her pushchair. 'Plastic is a real problem in the oceans now. How about this instead?' I pointed to a 'wildlife friendly' shrub in a pot.

'This is much greener. We can plant it in the

garden and you could look at it every day!'

Lily shook her head and pouted. 'I'm

not sure that's a good idea,' interjected

Mum wearily, moving the plant away from

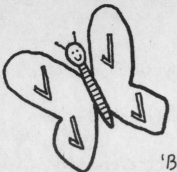

my sister, who was considering eating it.

'But look, it says it's good for butterflies!' I said, pointing to a large butterfly-shaped sticker on the pot. Lily is **really** into butterflies right now. A few weeks ago it was trains, and next week it will be something completely different, but at the moment, it's butterflies. Once she'd seen the sticker, she really wanted it.

Mum sighed and put the plant in her

trolley. She had more boring shopping to do,

so I went off to look round the shops on my

own for a bit.

'Did you buy anything with your pocket

money, Max?' asked Mum on the way home.

'Er . . . nothing much, really,' I replied,

looking out of the grimy bus window. I half-

crossed my fingers behind my back, because

this was only half-true.

In my bedroom back home, I pulled out the bag I'd stuffed in my pocket, and took out the contents. I *had* bought something, but it *wasn't much*—it was on special offer. I'd seen a Gerbil Hero! action figure, and couldn't resist. Kids collect them at school—Martin Williams in the class above has eight!—and I thought I should start a collection. Buying it had cheered me up, and it

Gerbil Hero!

was pretty cool. Now though, as I turned the figure over in my hands, it seemed a lot less cool. I'd stopped Mum buying a plastic toy for Lily, but then I'd gone and bought a plastic thing for myself. I wondered what Nish was doing right now—if I could tell him about it he'd laugh about this for sure.

It started to really bother me. With fingers <u>fully-crossed</u> behind my back this time, I told Mum I was going to the park to meet friends, but got the bus into town again.

I took the Gerbil Hero! back to the shop,

got a refund, and spent it on a collection

of bluebell bulbs in the plant shop. Then, I

walked to school. I knew where there was

a hole in the fence, so I could get to the

Forest of Hope. I felt like a total

loser sneaking into school on a Sunday,

especially when I ripped my jeans crawling

through the fence. I planted the bulbs as

quickly as possible, in case someone saw

me and thought I was burying a body or

something. But no one came, and it felt like

I'd done the right thing.

A few days later, Ms Perkins told me that she'd agreed that Nish's mum could come into school to demonstrate her vegetarian food. All my class were going to come. I was excited!

Mrs Gupta arrived at the start of the

lunch break, and I helped her carry the food to our classroom. I thought Nish might help too, but I couldn't find him. There was so much food, and my mouth was watering— there were tubs of curry and rice, jars of pickles, samosas, and a box of homemade sweets. There were even recipes to take away and try at home.

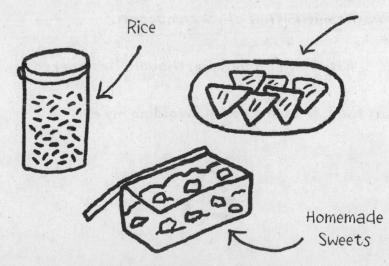

Samosas

Rice

Homemade Sweets

Ms Perkins brought the rest of the class over, and there were soon crowds of kids buzzing around trying all the dishes, and jostling to scoop up the sweets. Mrs Gupta was loving it, talking to everyone, explaining about the ingredients and giving out recipe cards. Everyone was really enjoying the yummy food, and even Tessa admitted that she wasn't missing her chicken nuggets.

Nish wasn't joining in, though. He lingered at the side of the room, avoiding my eye

and sulkily nibbling on a

chapati. His mum saw

him, and called him over.

'What are you doing,

Nishant? Aren't you hungry? You used

to love cooking with me at home.' Nish

reluctantly dragged himself over to the

table. 'That reminds me—look at these!'

she continued, reaching into her bag to pull

out a photo album.

'Don't, Mum!' Nish exclaimed, but it was

too late. She'd opened the album and was

showing everyone the pictures. They were all

of Nish, about three years old, in the kitchen

with his mum. I leaned forward to look. There

he was, grinning a toothy smile and stirring

something in a bowl.

'Ooh, cute,' someone

said. About twenty kids

were clustered round Mrs

Gupta, tittering with mouths full of food

as she flicked through the photos.

'He was always so keen to help me in the

kitchen, but now he's not interested,' she

sighed.

'Put it away, please!' Nish pleaded,

but there was no

stopping his mum.

'Ah, this one's my favourite.' She held up a picture of young Nish waving a spoon,  wearing a little apron with 'MUMMY'S LITTLE HELPER' on the front in bold letters. He didn't appear to be wearing anything else. I was feeling bad on Nish's behalf now. I turned to look for him, but he was striding towards the door. I started to follow him, but he gave me a look as he left the room that told me to leave him alone.

As we helped Mrs Gupta tidy up at the end, there was no doubt that it had been a success—her cookery had been a brilliant advert for vegetarian food. However, I couldn't shake the feeling that Nish was now really unhappy. I needed to talk to him.

I found Nish skulking in a corner of the playground, but before I had a chance to say anything he turned on me, eyes flashing with anger. 'You went too far this time Max!

161

You should have known I didn't want you to get my mum into school—she carries that photo album around with her everywhere, and I knew it was only a matter of time before she pulled it out.'

'But I . . . I just didn't think . . .'

I began, but Nish cut me short.

'You never do! That's your problem, Max! Get lost!' He marched off to join the others playing football.

I found Tessa at the other side of the playground. I was hoping she'd try to calm Nish down, but she didn't see it that way. 'I'm not surprised he's cross with you. How would you have felt? You should *totally* have asked Nish before getting his mum into school!'

'I didn't know she would embarrass Nish like that!' I explained, but Tessa wouldn't listen. 'I'll tell you who's embarrassing, Max —YOU!' With that, she turned and walked away.

I'd had a big row with my best friends and

they were blanking me, so I didn't feel like

being in the playground. I went off on my

own to look at the Forest of Hope,

thinking it would cheer me up. It did the

opposite—I was dismayed to see that some

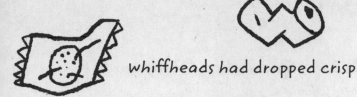 whiffheads had dropped crisp

packets and pop cans around the

bottom of the trees. I picked it

all up and headed back to lessons,

past windows wide open despite the cold, and

lights burning energy in empty classrooms.

I put the trash in the recycling point.

Rubbish, rubbish, rubbish! What

difference had we actually made?

The rest of the day really dragged, and I

was so relieved when it was finally time to go

165

home. As I was leaving, I saw Nish near the

school gates, but he refused to look at me.

I really needed to try and sort things out.

I walked over hesitantly, gulped, and said

Nish, I'm sorry I upset you. You see—

He blocked my path with

his hand. 'Not now. My

mum's taking me in

the car to my karate

class. She'll be here

any minute.'

'Er . . . what about the **Car-Free Campaign?**' I frowned. **'Shut up, Max!'**

he shouted back. 'I'm so fed up of you telling everyone what to do all the time. You're like Brussel sprouts — green and really boring! I'm always there, helping you with your grand plans, but you never seem to see that when things go wrong, it affects me too!'

Mrs Gupta's car arrived, and he stomped

off without looking back, slamming the car door as he got in. They drove off, leaving me alone at the side of the road. I sighed, and set off to walk.

I arrived at home feeling lower than a worm's belly button. I walked into the lounge to find the TV and lights on, but no one in there. Mum and Dad were in the kitchen. The heating was on full blast, but they'd opened the windows, letting all the heat escape.

'Hello! How was school?' asked Mum, and I just scowled in reply. 'Oh dear . . . one of those days? Come on, I'll make you a cuppa,' she offered, filling the kettle.

'Hey, you don't need to fill it right up!' I exclaimed. 'All the lights are on, and the heating. You're always going on about saving money, but look how much energy you're wasting! Do you even care?'

Escaping heat

Highest setting

She gave me a look and put the kettle down. 'Give it a rest, OK? I've had a rough day too. It would be nice if you weren't on our case about this *all* the time.'

Yes, stop lecturing us, Max. I get more than enough of that from my boss at work.

I was really fed up. Fed up with everyone, and `EVERYTHING!` 'Forget the tea. I'll go to my room,' I announced.

Alone in my bedroom, I hoped I'd be able

to distract myself with computer games, or

reading books, or *anything*; but my thoughts

kept returning to the disastrous day I'd had,

both at school and when I arrived home.

I turned the day's events over in my mind.

I'd thought I was starting to get somewhere

with my **Plan for the Planet**,

but now I was having serious doubts. Even

worse was the creeping feeling that even if I

did make the changes I wanted to see, I'd lose

my friends and fall out with my parents in the process. Would that be worth it? The more I thought about it, the more dismayed I felt.

I went to bed early that night, hoping that everything would feel better in the morning. Unfortunately, it didn't. I woke up far too early, my head spinning with worries like a washing machine full of dog poo, and I knew I wouldn't get back to sleep.

I wanted to get out of the house. I got dressed quickly and tiptoed into the kitchen, which seemed so empty without the usual bustle. I saw the family photo on the fridge, with Lily grinning like a gap-toothed goblin at the front. She was so little, really, and it was her future I'd been trying to save too—and all our futures. It shouldn't be this hard!

I picked up a notepad and pen from the side, and sat down to write. I left a note on the table, and slipped out of the house into the cold morning.

Dear Mum, Dad and Lily,

I'm sorry I annoyed you and you think I'm always telling you all what to do, and that I hid the car keys and keep turning the heating down. And I'm sorry I had a wee in the bath to save water. Actually, maybe you didn't know about that, but, anyway, I won't do it again. It was a bit weird.

I've been doing all this because I'm really worried about the future. (I don't mean the weeing in the bath—I did that because I

Do this.

Do that.

???

couldn't be bothered to get out.) Climate

change all feels so horrible, and trying to

change things makes it less scary, so I'm

determined to do what I can.

    I thought that if everyone got together we

could make a difference, but it seems I'm just

falling out with my friends AND my family.

 I can't keep going like this.

I'm really sorry about all the trouble

I've caused.

    Love, Max

I stomped away from the house. I didn't

want to be at home, but I didn't want to go

to school either. What was the point? It felt

like all my campaigning, all my planning, was

a waste of time, and was making everyone

unhappy—my friends, my family, and, most

of all, me. I'd started all this because I

thought people could help change the world

<u>TOGETHER</u>, but all I seemed to be

doing was driving people away from me,

and I felt very alone.

Suddenly, a bicycle bell tinkled

behind me—well, at least someone

was out of their car. The bell kept dinging,

and I turned round, to see Mum and Dad

on their tandem, with Lily perched on the

little seat at the back. They must have left

in a hurry, as they were still wearing their

pyjamas, and their cycle helmets. A strange

combination, but better than their *hideous*

bin bag outfits.

> Hey Max—glad we caught you!

exclaimed Mum, as they wobbled

to a stop next to me. 'We read your letter and

came straight out. We're really sorry you're

feeling so downhearted. We know things have

been difficult, but we're not angry with you!'

'Here, you left without having your

breakfast!' Dad added, passing me some

toast and jam from the back of the tandem.

'In a reusable lunchbox, too!' he grinned.

179

'Don't think we're not supportive of what you're trying to do, Love. We're really proud of you! No one gets everything right first time, but we know you're just worried about the future and are trying to make a difference. We're behind you all the way, you know, and we're going to try to make some changes ourselves, too.'

Mum reached over the handlebars and gave me a big hug. 'It will all be OK, Max. We're on your side! Now, you'd better get to school, and we'd better get home and get

ready for work. We'll see you later. Come on,

don't just stand there—you've got a planet to

save!' She winked, and they rode off, waving

and smiling. I walked on towards school,

and I felt as if they'd taken a weight off my

shoulders.

And my jammy toast didn't
weigh me down for long...

My head was clearer by the time I got to

school, because I'd made up with Mum and

Dad, and had eaten the toast Dad had given

me. Breakfast always helps! I felt myself

tense up again at the school gates, though,

because I was worried about seeing my

friends. Were they even still my friends?

I trudged into school, head down. I felt

a tap on the shoulder, and turned to see

Nish and Tessa. We all stood there looking at

each other, saying nothing, until I broke the

silence.

↑ Tumbleweed

I took a deep breath, and then

words flooded out of me.

I'm sorry! I know I've

cheesed you both off. I'm

not surprised you don't want

to hang out with me any more, if all I do

these days is annoy you. I don't blame you if

you've had enough of bossy old Mr Brussel

Sprouts!

To my surprise, they both laughed.

'It's OK,' said Nish. 'You really wound me

up and I was angry, which is why I shouted at

you. I'm just about over it—just promise you'll

never drag my mum into your schemes

again!'

'I promise!' I said. 'I know I get carried

away sometimes, but I've learned my lesson.'

'I hope so, Max! I'll admit that we've

missed you,' smiled Nish ruefully.

When Tessa and I walked to school this morning,

it just felt wrong without you chatting away

about your <u>bonkers</u> <u>plans.</u>

185

'You might be annoying sometimes, Max, but you're our best friend, and that's what really matters,' added Tessa. 'If you didn't do all this crazy stuff, you wouldn't be **you**. We wouldn't change you . . . not for all the trees in the world!'

'I think all the trees in the world are worth a lot more than me,' I mused. 'If you have to choose between saving me or a rainforest, it's the forest every time!'

'Leave it out,' laughed Nish, slapping

me on the back. 'We'll settle for saving you

AND the rainforests! Now, come on or

we'll be late.' Tessa put her arm through

mine, and we walked together towards the

classroom.

As we took our places for the register I
sat there happily, feeling a wave of relief run
over me like a warm shower (which uses less
water than a bath, by the way). Having good
friends in the world is another thing that
makes the planet worth saving.

As Ms Perkins was running

through the register, there

was a knock on the door,

and Mr Costive burst

in, waving a piece

of paper. He looked

flustered, and clearly

something was up. He was

looking at me! I felt a stab of

dread, as if my warm shower had suddenly

turned icy cold. Was I in trouble again?

The classroom had gone deathly quiet.

'Sorry to interrupt, Ms Perkins, but you should hear this. You sent off an entry to a competition with, um,'—he looked at the paper in his hand—

Wilf's Wacky Weekend Wig-out.

Anyway, it seems the school won! They're giving us an award, and there will be a special assembly this afternoon to present it!

Nobody could concentrate for the rest of the

morning. Everyone was distracted in lessons,

and at breaktime it was all anyone talked

about. There was a rumour going around

that Wilf himself was going to turn up in a

helicopter, which I kind of hoped **was** true

191

because that would be so awesome, and kind
of hoped **wasn't** because a bike would be
much more environmentally friendly.

I was in too much of a daze to feel
excited yet. When people kept congratulating
me, it just didn't seem real. Only when the
TV crew arrived in a very shiny van did it
start to sink in. The campaigning had all been
worthwhile. WE'D DONE IT!

Everyone filed into the assembly hall,

jostling for spaces near the front, where the

TV people were scurrying around, setting

up microphones, lights, and big cameras.

Mr Costive was standing on the stage,

talking to a woman with a clipboard.

Then, she swapped her clipboard for a

microphone, turned round and addressed the

hall, which was now full, and asked for quiet.

An expectant hush fell over the hall. The

curtains at the back of the room parted . . .

and in came WILF, just like on the TV

(although he looked smaller

in real life). The room

erupted as he walked to

the front of the stage,

took the microphone,

and started speaking.

'Hey, everyone! How are we feeling?' he

said, to another huge cheer. 'It's great to

visit Jedley School today to present this

award for all your tree-mendous work—

TREE-mendous, get it? Hey,

Mr Costive, you must be very proud!'

'Er, yes!' answered the Mr Costive,

nervously. 'I run a good school.'

'It's certainly a GREEN school—and

this is why we chose you for this fantastic

award!' said Wilf to more cheers, taking a

card from his pocket. He started reading out

all the things that we'd achieved, to cheers

every time . . . 'Transport campaign!

HOORAY! Tree-planting and

wildlife area! HOORAY! Energy-

saving insulation! HOORAY!

You've done more in a short time

than any other school in the country,

and that's why we're giving you the

Wilf's Wonderful World
Award! We're going to take the whole

school on a special wildlife activity day as a

reward!'

Amidst fresh waves of cheering,

clipboard woman passed Wilf a box, from

which he took a shiny trophy in the shape of

the globe, about the size of a tennis ball. He

197

gave it to a bemused Mr Costive.

'A few words, Mr Costive?

What made you keen to make

your school green?'

'Er . . . well, this is a lovely surprise,'

he stuttered, peering suspiciously into the

camera. 'We . . . um . . . do good things here

under my leadership.

I'm a big ideas person!' (He broke

into a weedy smile now—a

rare event.)

'It's fitting that our hard work has been rewarded. This fine trophy will have pride of place in my office!' he said, enthusiastically shaking hands with Wilf for the cameras.

I couldn't believe it—'<u>our</u>' hard work, he said! Sitting here watching Mr Costive grinning like a ninny on the stage felt really strange. I was used to mixed feelings—they'd been mixed up ever since that night of bad dreams and everything that followed. I was so pleased that we'd started to green up the school, and won a NATIONAL AWARD for it. Mr Costive pretending it was all his idea was just wrong, though. He'd not helped at all while we tried to get things done, and now look at him! Why do the people in charge always take the credit for other people's hard work?

Suddenly, there was a commotion (and for once, it wasn't me making it). It was Tessa, next to me, standing up, and everyone turned to look.

'Excuse me sir! You've forgotten something, sir. None of this would have happened if it wasn't for my friend Max.' She

spoke strongly, but I could see that her hands

were shaking.

On my other side, Nish stood up to join

her. That's right, sir. This was Max's idea all

along. If he hadn't nagged everyone till he

was blue in the face, we'd never have gone

green.

NAG.

NAG.

NAG.

NAG.

Teal blue
#008081

A ripple of nervous laughter spread

across the hall. On stage, Wilf looked first at

Mr Costive with raised eyebrows, then back at

me. - - - - - - - - → 😊 ← Now turning red

Then Ms Perkins stood up too, at the

front. 'If I may quickly say something, Mr

Costive. The children have a point. Max

Twyford filled out the application for this

award, and he initiated most of the green

improvements. If it wasn't for him, I'm sure

we wouldn't have won.'

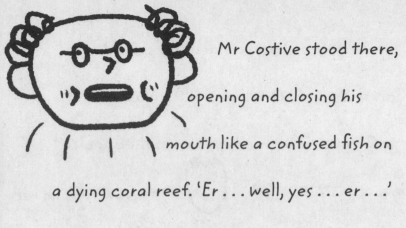

Mr Costive stood there, opening and closing his mouth like a confused fish on a dying coral reef. 'Er... well, yes... er...' he blustered.

'Hey, let's hear from this Max!' said Wilf, grinning his TV grin. 'Where are you? What have you got to say?'

I felt hundreds of eyes on me, and Tessa and Nish pulling me up out of my seat. 'Come on, stand up!' they whispered. Time suddenly

seemed to be going very slowly. I got to my

feet, and **everyone** was looking at

me. One of the TV cameras at the front

had swivelled round, and Wilf was pointing

straight at me.

'There he is! Come on, gang—let's have a

Wacky Wilf's Wahoo for Max!' He yelled, and

all the kids cheered:

WAHOOOOOO! The clapping

and shouting went on for ages, and everyone

joined in, even those kids who'd moaned

about walking to school. Even grumpy Danny

Belter looked happy! I could see Ms Perkins

smiling broadly, while Mr Costive managed a

false grin. WOBBLY LIPS

'Happy-wacky days, Max! Tell everyone

how you're feeling!' said Wilf, when the

cheering subsided. One of the TV crew

came over, and passed

a microphone to me.

The room went quiet, as

hundreds of pairs of eyes plus

two cameras looked straight at me.

My mind flashed back to my speech in

front of the mirror with the shampoo bottle,

but words wouldn't come out. I felt a gentle

kick from Nish. I had to say something!

'Umm . . . yes, it WAS my plan to make

the school greener,' I began. 'But, on my own

I couldn't have done much. I was feeling all alone and like no one else cared, but then lots of other kids joined the campaign and tried to make things better. Parents and some teachers helped too, and my friends have been especially awesome, thank you! At times, I'll admit I felt like giving up— but I'm so glad I kept trying to do the right thing, even if it wasn't always easy and I messed it up sometimes. It shows we can be stronger and actually change things when we act _together_!'

There was another round of applause

from the hall. 'Well, well! That's just terrific,

Max. Thank you and well done everyone!'

said Wilf. The TV guy held his hand out for

the mic.

'Hang on, I've got more

to say!' I continued,

not nervous anymore.

I climbed up onto

my chair, raised my

arms, and addressed my audience. 'Hello everyone! Smile, we're on TV!' I heard Mr Costive tutting, but laughter spreading through the hall drowned him out. I continued, 'Remember that I started all this because I was worried about climate change ruining our future. What we've done is great, but it's not enough. It's not just this school that needs to change, but EVERYTHING.'

The hall had fallen silent. Hundreds of

people were really listening to me, and I was

on actual TV! I was tingling with excitement,

and suddenly knew what I had to say. 'Maybe

you've heard about the climate strike

happening around the world, with kids like us

protesting for real change, and our future—'

Mr Costive cut in suddenly, from the stage.

'Yes, thank you Max, that was

MOST interesting. Now, I think—'

I continued, ignoring the interruption—

I had the microphone, not him! 'Sometimes

the people in charge only listen if you make

a REAL fuss. It's time to make a fuss!

I'm going to walk out and start our very own

climate strike, today. Who's with

me?'

It was now or never. I dropped the mic,

and headed towards the door. I looked

back and saw a sea of faces watching me in

silence as I stood alone at the edge of the

room. I felt a twinge of panic—had I just

made the biggest fool of myself, on TV?

The hall filled with a low

murmuring of voices.

Tessa and Nish looked

at each other, then

stood up together, and

came to stand with

me. The chatter in the hall

grew louder, and became

a storm of noise, with

the scraping of chairs

being pushed back, and the

clamour of hundreds

of excited kids. We were on

the move!

Mr Costive's

voice cut through:

'Be quiet!

Unacceptable—sit down!'
but he had no chance of
stopping the growing tide of
cheering kids. The strike was
on! I felt giddy with excitement,
and a little scared. We were taking a stand,
and who knew what would happen? As we
burst out into the sunny playground, I didn't
know—but I knew it felt right.

THE END.

WALK
& CYCLE MORE

And if you need to go far, share your journey.

Cars produce a lot of carbon dioxide. We get happier and healthier when we walk and cycle too. If we share the car or use buses and trains, we pollute the world less.

BUY LESS
& LOOK AFTER WHAT YOU'VE GOT

A lot of modern things are made of oil. For example, all plastic and many of the clothes you wear come from oil products. But one day, the oil will run out.

Think before you buy. Do you really need that new thing? It is better to mend things and swap or share with your friends than to throw them away and buy new.

TURN DOWN THE HEAT
& PUT ON A JUMPER

Heating houses produces a lot of carbon dioxide. If we feel cold, we can put on an extra jumper. We can also turn off the radiator and lights when we are not using a room, and turn the TV off standby when we are not watching it.

These pages were written by Mim Saxl, Low Carbon West Oxford & Eleanor Watts, Rose Hill & Iffley Low Carbon

PROTECT NATURE
& PLANT MORE TREES

We need trees because they suck in carbon dioxide and give out oxygen, which we need to breathe! Planting trees and looking after the animals around us is a good thing—and can be a lot of fun!

TALK ABOUT YOUR FEELINGS
& TAKE ACTION

A lot of us feel scared or worried about climate change. It helps to talk about how you feel with family and friends. Maybe they'll want to make some changes too! You could make notices for the playground, ask your parents to walk you to school or write to your MP.

EAT LESS MEAT & DAIRY
& BUY LOCAL FOOD

In many parts of the world, people are cutting down or burning trees so that they can raise animals for meat. Also, cows, sheep, and pigs burp and fart a lot. This produces methane, which is a powerful greenhouse gas!

Some of the story ideas were inspired by the work Kids Climate Action Network are doing.

You can visit the website here: kidsclimateaction.org

Tim Allman grew up in Worcestershire, where unfortunately he was nowhere near as clued-up about green issues as children are today. He studied botany and nature conservation at university and then left a perfectly adequate job to run away and join the anti-roadbuilding protests. This led to a decade spent as a full-time environmental activist, and a life-long commitment to working for social and environmental change.

Nick Shepherd comes from a small industrial village in Yorkshire, and with the rolling green countryside only a short bike ride away, he would enjoy nothing more than staying indoors, playing video games, and drawing silly characters. Years of study and work later, and not much has changed. Nick is an animal lover; he once rescued two baby squirrels and nursed them back to full health. Now he shares his home and art studio with his cat, who will happily spend the whole day sat on his keyboardddddddd.